THE MYSTERIOUS SEA BUNNY

written and illustrated by
Peter Raymundo

 Dial Books for Young Readers

Gather around, children.
We are about to observe something you have
never seen before.

Today we are going to follow the mysterious . . .
sea bunny.

You could say that. But please say it *quietly*.
It doesn't know we're watching.

WHOA! What's all that . . . STUFF?

I thought you said you'd be qui—oh, never mind. You must mean the sea bunny's trail of slime.

Slime? I've made slime before!

Not like this you haven't. The sea bunny makes *this* slime with its own body.

You should *never* judge a slug by its slime.
This mucus does all kinds of things, like letting
the sea bunny crawl wherever it wants.

Sea Bunny can even crawl

UPSIDE DOWN

if it needs to.

Wow! Are there suction cups on its feet or something?

Well, no and no.
Sea slugs don't have suction cups.
And they don't have feet either.

But they do have a FOOT.

foot

And it's strong too. In fact, by rippling the muscles in its foot, a sea bunny can crawl up to fifty feet an hour.

That's not far, is it?

That's because sea bunnies are only one inch long.

That's like the size of a quarter!

It is indeed. And being so small has HUGE benefits, like the ability to hide just about anywhere.

I bet it's great at hide-and-seek!

That's true, especially in the dark.

Sea slugs' eyes are so small, they mostly see blurry light and shadows.

The fact is, some things just aren't what they seem.
Kind of like how this looks like a cute, fluffy bunny tail.

But these are actually the sea bunny's gills.

Gills are what the sea bunny uses to breathe.

What? No. They breathe through their gills that happen to be on the back side of their bodies. Moving on.

No, no. Sponges are a sea bunny's favorite food, especially the poisonous ones.

Wait. A *poisonous* sponge?

Yep. If you look closely, you can see the sea bunny sucking in tiny bits of spo—

We have just witnessed the sea bunny's greatest power.
By eating the poisonous sponge, the sea bunny
became poisonous himself.

A mystery indeed. What is more mysterious
than a slug that looks like a bunny?

Dozens of sea slugs.

Wait! There's no way all of these are slugs!

There is a way. Sea Bunny is just one of the MANY shapes, sizes, and colors that sea slugs come in.

Oh, I can be quiet!

Sigh. I'm sure you can.

**Dedicated to Dorothy, Andrew, and Mr. Plume,
who were there every inch of the way.**

DIAL BOOKS FOR YOUNG READERS
An imprint of Penguin Random House LLC, New York

First published in the United States of America by Dial Books for Young Readers, an imprint of Penguin Random House LLC, 2021

Copyright © 2021 by Peter Raymundo

Visit us online at penguinrandomhouse.com.

Library of Congress Cataloging-in-Publication Data is available.
Manufactured in China • ISBN 9780593325148
1 3 5 7 9 10 8 6 4 2

Design by Jennifer Kelly • Text set in Avenir Next and Dom Casual
The artwork in this book was drawn and painted on a Wacom Cintiq using the amazing Photoshop brushes created by Kyle T Webster.